Arabba Gah Zee, Marissa and Me!

Story and pictures by
Ruth Rosner

Albert Whitman & Company, Niles, Illinois

Text and illustrations © 1987 by Ruth Rosner
Published in 1987 by Albert Whitman & Company, Niles, Illinois
Published simultaneously in Canada by General Publishing, Limited, Toronto
All rights reserved. Printed in the United States of America.
10 9 8 7 6 5 4 3 2 1

Library of Congress Cataloging-in-Publication Data

Rosner, Ruth.
Arabba gah zee, Marissa and me!

Summary: Two friends with vivid imaginations play at
being spies, ballerinas, rock stars, pirates, and
sisters, having so much fun that they never want to
stop.
[1. Play—Fiction. 2. Imagination—Fiction]
I. Title.
PZ7.R71955Ar 1987   [E]   86-15904
ISBN 0-8075-0442-4

This book is dedicated
to Rachel
and her friends.

When I ask Marissa to play after school,
she asks her mom.

If the answer is yes, and it almost always is,
Marissa calls, "Laura, RUN!
We're being followed by spies!"

We race down the steep path past the school.
Our mothers take the sidewalk.

When they meet up with us and ask,
"How was school?" or "What did you have for lunch?"
we pretend we don't understand English.
Marissa says something like, "Arabba gah zee,"
which is supposed to mean "Quick! Up the wall!"
I say, "Owamba la bah," which means "Wait for me!"

From the top of the wall, we can see my building.
Whoever spots it first shouts, "Head for the hideout!"

Marissa protects me from the robots out front.
I yell "SAFE!" when I touch the door.

You have to say the secret word
if you want to get into the elevator.
Marissa's is "caterpillars" and mine is "swordfish."
Then you push the button three times and wait
for the door to open.

If the spies follow us in, we disguise ourselves.
Usually we're famous ballerinas from the
Royal Ballet at Covent Garden.
We do arabesques and grand pliés until the
elevator gets to my floor.

Then we leap out the door to safety.
Sometimes Marissa gets the key and sometimes I do.
We sneak it away while the spies are busy talking.

Inside the hideout, we eat.

We're soooooo hungry.

We like green apples and green grapes better than tangerines.

Marissa says cookies with filling give secret powers.

I say the plain ones can turn you into monsters.

We only take drinks that fizz.

As soon as we're done, we change into show clothes.
Marissa's favorite colors are purple and pink.
Mine are pink and red.

We pretend we're French gymnasts who do exercise to music.
I'm ZSA ZSA. Marissa is GIGI.
The audience sits on the couch—
unless we get them to join us.

If we change into rock stars,
Marissa wears the red boa. I get the feathers.
We always serve hors d'oeuvres after the show.

If we don't know what to play next,
we try on clothes until we get an idea—
like playing sisters who are teenagers.

I'm Sherry and I usually break my arm and wear a cast.
Marissa is Shelley and she breaks her leg and needs crutches.
Sometimes we fight over the crutches.
We always fight over the wheelchair.

Once when that happened, I got so mad I left the room
and turned on the television.
Another time, Marissa took a book into the bathroom
and slammed the door.

Today when we started to fight,
Marissa said, "Let's be pirates instead."
"Great!" I said. "We can duel."
I was just leaping over the ocean from my boat to Marissa's
when our mothers walked in.
"NO WATER IN THE LIVING ROOM!" they shouted.

So we quit that game, and I said,
"Let's be sisters who are twins who get carried
away by monsters who trap us in a cave."

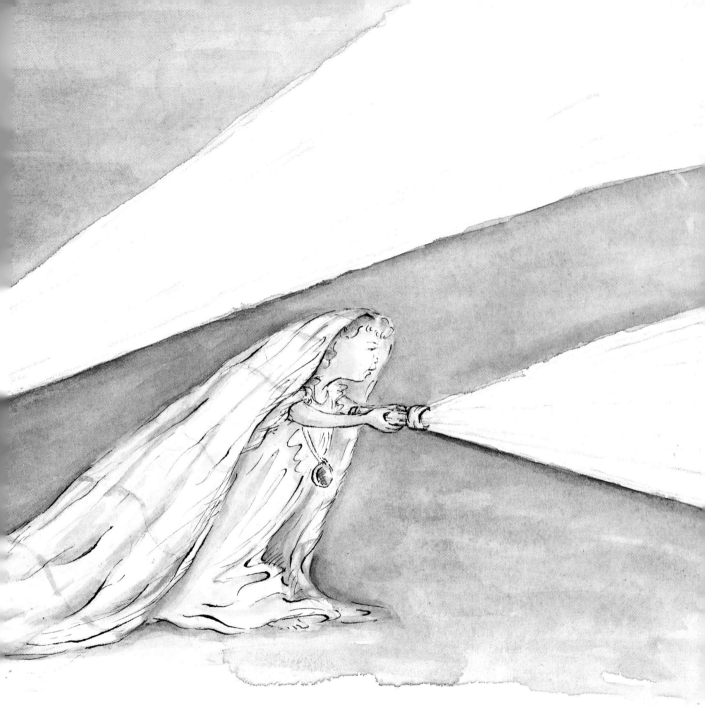

The only way we could escape was to hide under blankets
and sneak away in the night.
It was a little too dark with the lights off and the shades down,
so we had to use flashlights and bicycle reflectors.

Then we ran home to our baby sisters,
who desperately needed baths and shampoos.

We left them to dry and made
a potion powerful enough to turn us invisible.
We mixed shampoos and soaps and toothpastes and
powder and food coloring that turned the potion a perfect purple.
We had just added the baking powder to make the whole thing bubble,
when we heard, "LAURA! MARISSA! TIME TO CLEAN UP!"

It was awful!
We had just started playing.
We begged for one more minute.

"AT THE COUNT OF TEN!" said our mothers.
And they began to count, just as they always do:
"ONE . . . TWO . . . THREE . . . FOUR . . ."

Marissa and I did just what *we* always do.
We hid.

But it was no use. We had to clean up.
We threw all the play clothes into the basket
and looked for Marissa's sneakers.

Then we had to say good-bye.
I thanked Marissa for coming.
And Marissa thanked me for the nice time.
She promised we could finish our game soon
at her house.

After Marissa left, I asked my mom
if she wanted to play ballerinas.

She was pretty good.
But no one's as good at playing as Marissa.

Marissa says the same thing
about me.